FRED BEAR and FRIENDS

AT THE
Hospital

By Melanie Joyce

WEEKLY READER®
PUBLISHING

Please visit our web site at www.garethstevens.com
For a free catalog describing our list of high-quality books,
call 1-800-542-2595 (USA) or 1-800-387-3178 (Canada).
Our fax: 1-877-542-2596

Library of Congress Cataloging-in-Publication Data

Joyce, Melanie.
    At the hospital / Melanie Joyce.—North American ed.
        p. cm.—(Fred Bear and friends)
    Summary: When Arthur fall off of his bike and hurts himself, Fred
accompanies him to the hospital for an examination and X-rays.
    ISBN-13: 978-0-8368-8970-3 (lib. bdg.)
    ISBN-10: 0-8368-8970-3 (lib. bdg.)
    ISBN-13: 978-0-8368-8977-2 (softcover)
    ISBN-10: 0-8368-8977-0 (softcover)
    [1. Hospitals — Emergency services — Fiction. 2. Medical
care — Fiction. 3. Teddy bears—Fiction. 4. Toys — Fiction.]
    I. Title.
PZ7.J8283Ath   2008
[E] —dc22   2007031338

This North American edition first published in 2008 by
Weekly Reader® Books
An Imprint of Gareth Stevens Publishing
1 Reader's Digest Road
Pleasantville, NY 10570-7000 USA

This U.S. edition copyright © 2008 by Gareth Stevens, Inc. Original edition
copyright © 2007 by ticktock Media Ltd., First published in Great Britain in
2007 by ticktock Media Ltd., Unit 2, Orchard Business Centre, North Farm
Road, Tunbridge Wells, Kent, TN2 3XF United Kingdom

Gareth Stevens Senior Managing Editor: Lisa M. Guidone
Gareth Stevens Creative Director: Lisa Donovan
Gareth Stevens Art Director: Alex Davis
Gareth Stevens Associate Editor: Amanda Hudson

Photo credits (t=top, b=bottom, c=center, l=left, r=right, bg=background)
All photography by Colin Beer of JL Allwork Photography except for
Photolibrary.com: 11r; Shutterstock: 22tr, 23.

Every effort has been made to trace the copyright holders for the photos
used in this book, and the publisher apologizes in advance for any
unintentional omissions. We would be pleased to insert the appropriate
acknowledgements in any subsequent edition of this publication.

Printed in the United States of America

1 2 3 4 5 6 7 8 9 10 09 08 07

Fred

Meet Fred Bear and Friends

Arthur

Betty

Jess

Arthur has fallen off of his bike!

He hurt his left arm. Arthur also bumped his head.

Arthur needs to go to the hospital.

Fred asks their neighbor, Mr. Dobbs, to drive him and Arthur to the hospital.

"Let's go right now!" says Mr. Dobbs.

Fred and Arthur
walk in to
the hospital.

They sit
in the
waiting room.

A nurse calls
Arthur's name.
"The doctor
is ready to
see you,"
says the
nurse.

7

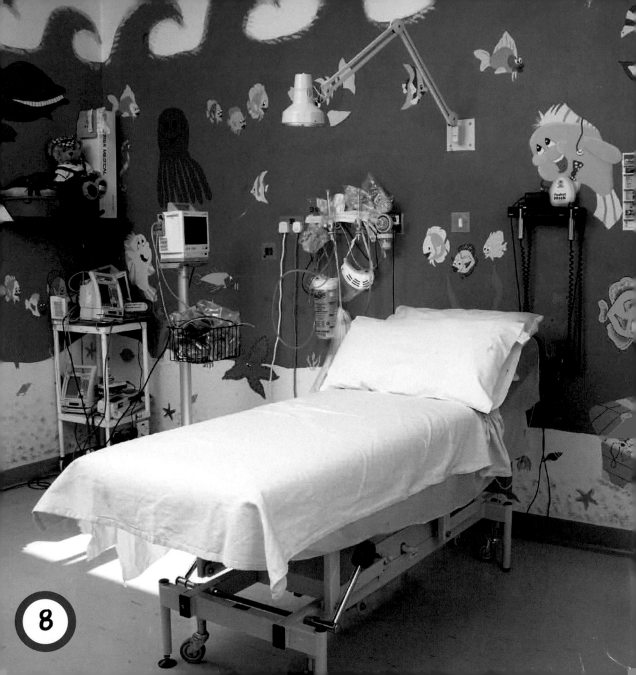

The nurse takes
Arthur and Fred into
a special room.

The nurse puts a
a name bracelet
on Arthur's arm.

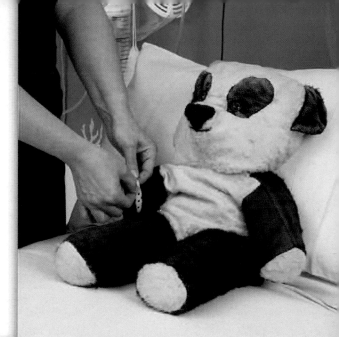

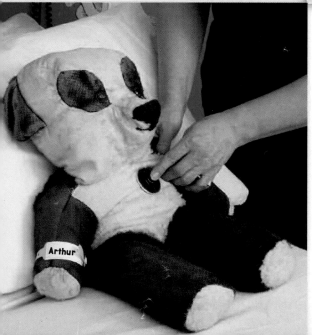

The doctor checks
Arthur's eyes and head.
She listens to his heart.

Thump, thump.

Then the doctor
checks Arthur's arm.
"You will need an
X-ray," she says.

9

Arthur feels dizzy. The nurse helps him into a wheelchair. She pushes him to the X-ray room.

In the X-ray room,
a special machine takes a
picture of Arthur's arm.
The picture is called an
X-ray. An X-ray shows the
doctor what is inside
Arthur's arm.

Fred Bear says...
X-rays are pictures that show
if bones are broken. This is
what an X-ray of your arm
and hand would look like.

The doctor shows the
X-ray to Arthur and Fred.

"You are lucky," says the
doctor. "Your arm is
not broken."

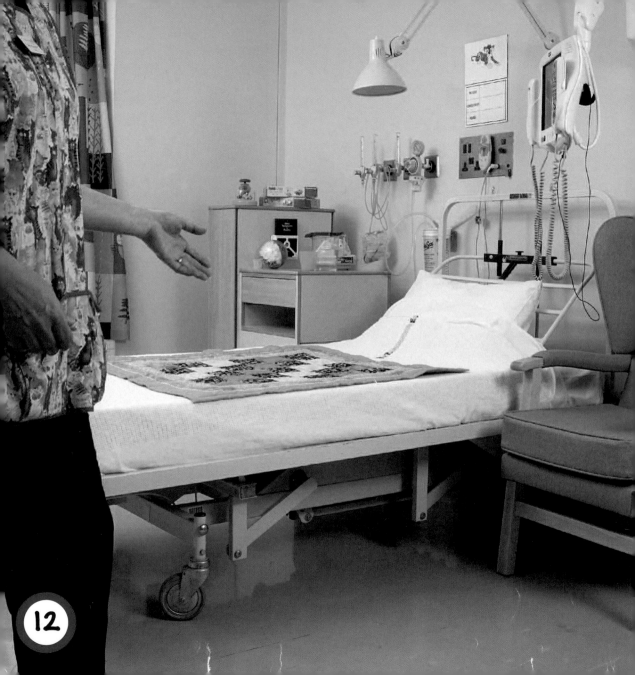

12

Arthur needs to sleep over at the hospital.

Fred has to leave. He knows the nurses will take good care of Arthur.

"Good-bye, Arthur," says Fred. "I will come back later."

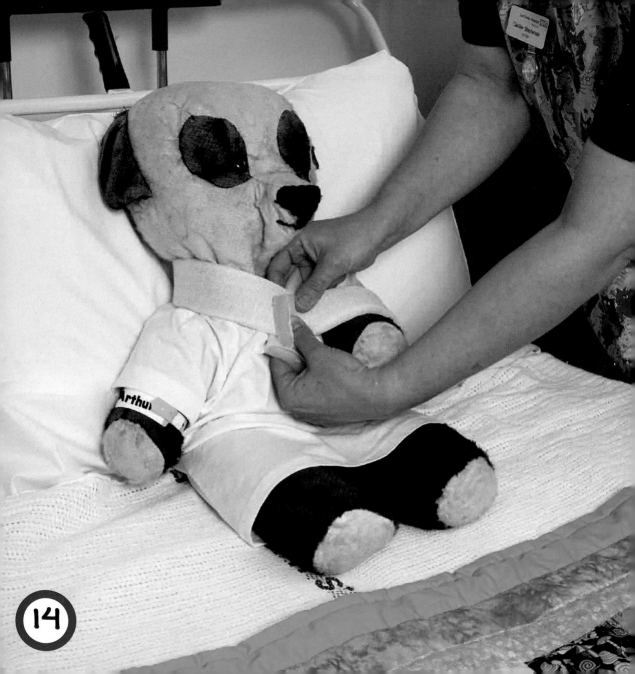

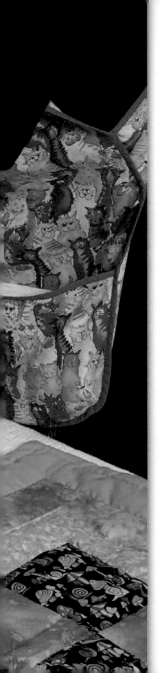

A nurse helps
Arthur put on
a hospital gown.
Then she puts his
arm in a sling.

A sling helps
Arthur's arm
feel better.

Later, Fred
comes back
to the hospital.
He has a present
for Arthur.

15

Arthur is happy to see Fred. He likes the big, red balloon.

After Fred's visit,
the nurse brings
Arthur's dinner.

Arthur likes to
to eat in bed!

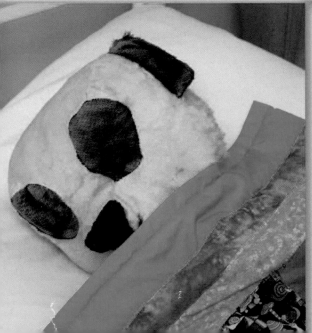

It was a long day.
Arthur is tired.
Soon he is asleep.

The next morning, the doctor checks Arthur's head and arm.

"You can go home now," says the doctor.

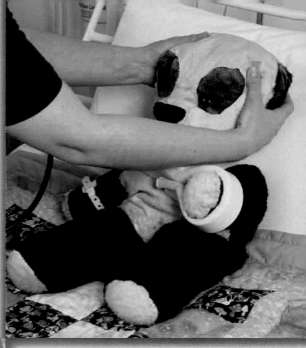

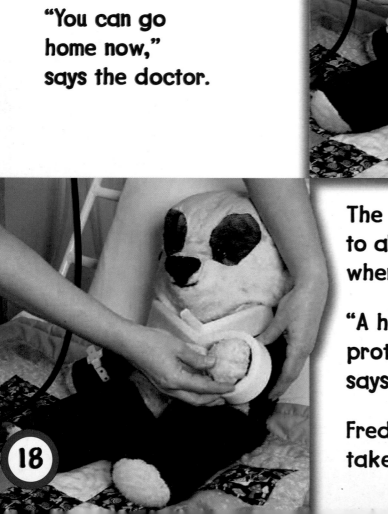

The doctor tells Arthur to always wear a helmet when he rides his bike.

"A helmet helps protect your head," says the doctor.

Fred and Mr. Dobbs take Arthur home.

18

Get Well Soon!

19

At home, Arthur tells his friends about the hospital.

They take turns playing doctor and patient.

Arthur is happy to be home again with his friends.

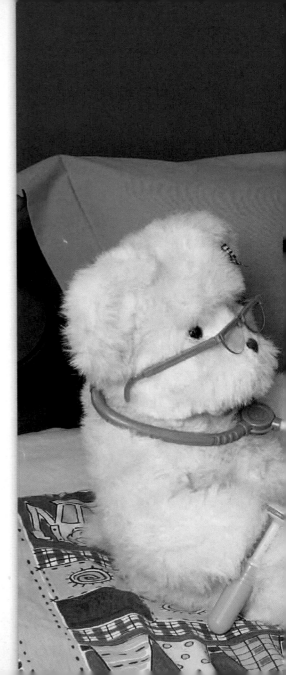

21

Safety Tips

Arthur went to the hospital because he got hurt.
Here are some tips to stay safe.

Roads

Always wear your helmet
when you ride your bike.

Look both ways before
you cross the road.

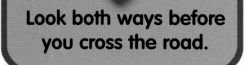

Always wear
a seat belt
in a car.

Home

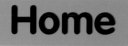

Never play with matches.
Fire is very harmful.

Hot drinks can burn you.
Do not touch a cup if you
think it is hot.

What are some
other ways
you stay safe?

Don't eat or
drink cleaning
products.

23

Match Parts of the Body

Look at the labels.
Point to each part
on Fred's body.